Love Grows LOVE

written by
Lauren Grabois Fischer

pictures by
Devin Hunt

The Be Books

www.TheBEbooks.com

I hope that you enjoy this book and the fun activities that follow after. If you come up with a great activity that promotes kindness, positivity, and love, and you want to share it with me, you can email your ideas to **lauren@thebebooks.com** or find me on social media **@thebebooks**!

You can follow my page for positive posts, updates on book giveaways, and new book releases. I would love to share your beautiful creations with others. You can have your parents or teachers post them on social media and tag **@thebebooks**. Make sure to use **#thebebooks** and **#laurengraboisfischer** in your posts.

Softcover - ISBN: 978-1-7333026-0-9
Hardcover - ISBN: 978-0-9862532-9-4

www.TheBEbooks.com
@theBEbooks

Printed in the USA
Signature Book Printing, www.sbpbooks.com

I want to dedicate this book to my grandparents and parents,
who taught me what true love is and that you get what you give. Through
infinite amounts of love and support, I have grown to be the person that
I am. I know that your patience, kindness, and love is what allowed me to
blossom into the writer that I am today. Thank you for reading my
endless amounts of poetry and for always believing that I have a gift
with words. You made me believe in myself and gave me the
confidence to write for others. I am forever grateful for that.

An extra special thank you to my Gramps Joseph for always collecting my
poetry and stories and reminding me that my words are a gift and that
they should be shared with others. Since I was young, you have always
made me feel special and smart, and you have taught me by example that
"Love Grows Love."

Love grows

LOVE

Smiles grow

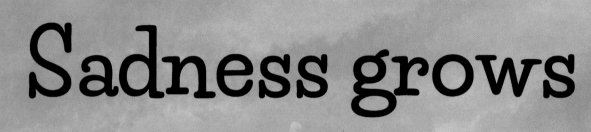

Sadness grows

Kindness grows

Fear grows

Laughter grows

LAUGHTER

Anger grows

Acceptance grows

Love grows

What will

you grow?

Dear Parents and Educators,

The idea of "Love Grows Love" came to me one day when I was spending time with my children. It became very clear to me that what we put in, we get back in return. The time, love, and energy that I share with my children transforms into their time, love, and energy that they want to share back with me. When I smile, they smile. When I laugh, they laugh with me. When I feel sad, I notice that they too feel sad. I had an "aha" moment and knew that it had to be turned into a children's book. After all, what is more powerful than the knowledge that what we do actually makes a difference? My actions and words can affect your day in a positive or negative way. My smile can cheer you up even if I don't know you. My "hello" may be the only friendly greeting that someone shares with you that day. If that is not power, I do not know what is. Let's use our power and our choices to help others. Through reading this book with your children/students and talking with them about the goodness that can come from them, I am hoping that more positive energy will flow through our world. Let us all focus on love and have a little less fear. Let us all smile more than cry. Let us be more accepting and a little less ignorant. Let us always know kindness and choose to ignore hate and anger. Let us find more LOVE that grows LOVE.

With love and gratitude,

Lauren Grabois Fischer

Inspiration & Discussion

· What is love? Is it something that we feel? Is it something that we see? Is it something that we know? Can love come in different forms?

· What is the opposite of love? Is it hate? Is it fear? Is it both?

· When you wake up in the morning, one of the first things that you should do is walk over to a mirror and look into your own eyes and say, "Good morning. I love you. Thank you for waking up." How can this change the direction of how your day may have gone? How can this ensure that you will have a beautiful day? Can your kindness to yourself really make you feel happy?

· Why is it important to smile at others? How can your smile affect someone else's day? Can it affect someone else's day?

· The word "hate" is a very strong word. Instead of using that word, let's try and use the word "dislike." For example, "I dislike my alarm clock." That sentence has a lot less negativity attached to it than it would if it used the word "hate." Come up with five sentences in which you would have said "hate," and switch it to "dislike." See if you feel better about the way that it sounds and feels.

- It is okay to feel sad. Everyone has something that will make them feel sad at one point. What is important is to recognize that you are feeling sad and be sympathetic to yourself. It is important that we be kind and patient with ourselves just as we would for another. Take the time to cry and heal. You can talk to someone who loves you, and they may even cheer you up. Another great idea is to write. Write your feelings down on paper. If you do not feel like writing, draw a picture, and see if that helps. Releasing those feelings onto paper is a very powerful thing. You naturally let go of some of the negativity holding on to you. Another important thing to remember is that sadness does not last forever. It is extremely important to remember not to stay there too long. There will ALWAYS be a reason to smile. There will ALWAYS be a reason to move forward. Find the happiness within because it is always there.

- Why is it important for us to be kind to others? How can we show kindness?

- Everyone is afraid of something. It could be something small or something big. Some people are afraid of heights while others love roller coasters. Some people are afraid of the dark while others love sleeping outdoors at night. We are all different, and we all feel differently. No one way is the right way. Do not judge someone else. Be aware that we all have different likes and dislikes. We all have different passions and fears. Be supportive of someone else who may be afraid of something that you are not. Help them and be a great friend. Talk with a partner about something that you are afraid of. Maybe your partner can help you find ways to be okay with it.

- How do you feel after you laugh?

- How can someone control his or her anger? What can we do to calm down in a moment where we feel frustrated?

- Why should we be accepting of others? What if they are different than us? Is that okay?

- What will you grow? Will it be peace? Will it be kindness? Think about it.

Activity Pages

· Go outside and pick five rocks from your front yard. If you do not have rocks, have your parents buy you some from a craft store. You will need the supplies listed below. Paint colorful designs on the rocks. Wait for them to dry. Once dry, use your permanent markers to write positive sayings on the rocks. It can be as simple as, "I love you," "You are beautiful," and/or "I am healthy." Once the rocks are dry and complete, find five special places in your neighborhood, city, or state to leave the rocks. The positive sayings will hopefully inspire someone to feel good and be kind to someone else.

Supplies:

5 rocks, paint and permanent markers.

· Play the "Kindness" game with your friends/classmates. The game is definitely more fun when lots of people play. You will need small sheets of paper and a pen for each person playing. You can also choose to speak aloud, but it is definitely more fun when each person gets to go home with a "kind" sheet of paper. The rules of the game:

1. Sit in a circle with all of your friends.
2. Write down on your piece of paper 2 positive things that you can say about the person to the left of you. If speaking out loud, this step is skipped.
3. Once everyone has come up with two nice things to say, take turns in the circle and read them out loud. When everyone is done reading, hand your paper to the person to your left. They can keep your kind words.

· "Acceptance" For this activity, you will need a partner. For a classroom setting, match up each student with another student. Every pair of students will answer the questions that follow the explanation. After everyone has met with their partner and answered all of the questions, the teacher will then ask if everyone had the same answers. The answer will most likely be no. This activity is to become aware of our differences and to recognize that being accepting of others is the best choice. Acceptance comes in all different ways. We do not need to look the same or think the same to be friends.

1. Where is your family originally from?
2. Where were you born?
3. What is your favorite kind of food?
4. What is your favorite thing to do?

- This game is called, "Throwing our fears into a bucket." A teacher or parent can be the leader of this game. You can find a real bucket in your home/classroom or you can use your imagination and simply use a cup. The person in charge will hand out 3 small sheets of paper (an index card is perfect) to each person. Everybody playing will be given 5-10 minutes to write down 3 things that they are afraid of. When each person is done writing, they will fold the paper in half and place it into the bucket. No one will be reading your words. They will stay in the bucket. This exercise is to try and release some of those fears and not have such a strong grip on them. You can have a conversation about letting things go and let the bucket be in charge of watching your fears.

- Laughter is one of the most amazing things! Take 5 minutes each day to have a "laughter party." The only thing that you have to do at this party is laugh. Get your friends and family to join in. It is very contagious. The ONLY rule for this game is to have fun and laugh!

· Draw a line of grass, on a blank piece of paper. What will you grow in your garden? Create a beautiful scene and write a few sentences about what you drew.

· Look in the mirror and name five things that you love about yourself.

1. _____

2. _____

3. _____

4. _____

5. _____

· **Gratitude List:** Use the lines below to write five things that you are grateful for.

1. _____

2. _____

3. _____

4. _____

5. _____

COLOR YOUR WORLD

I hope that after reading this book, you are feeling inspired!

Here is the chance for you to add your own style to your new favorite book!

Using CRAYONS only, fill in the pictures with the colors

that make your heart happy.

I can't wait to see what you have created! Take pictures of your BEAUTIFUL,

UNIQUE, and ONE OF A KIND creations and post it on social media.

Tag @thebebooks and I will share YOUR CREATION on my stories!

Do not rip out the pages from this book.

If you want more FREE coloring pages, visit my website

www.thebebooks.com for FREE downloads of all of my COLORING pages.

Thank you for COLORING OUR WORLD!

Love grows

Smiles grow

Kindness grows

Laughter grows

LAUGHTER

Acceptance grows

ACCEPTANCE

Love grows

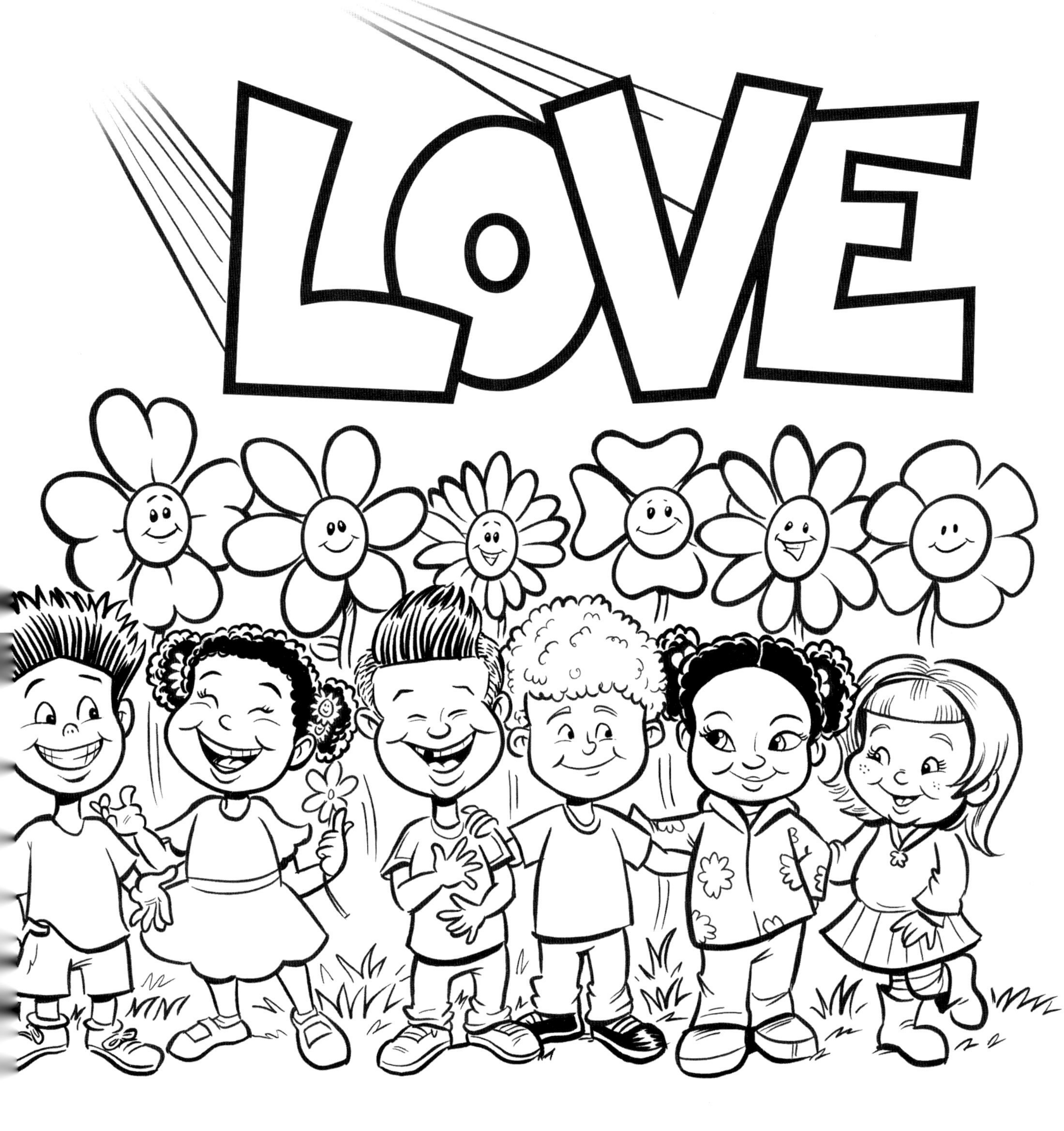
LOVE

I am so thankful for you! Thank you so much for taking the time to read,

"Love Grows Love." I believe that if we put our focus onto positivity and love, this

world will be a more happy and kind place. I feel so grateful and blessed that you have

taken time out of your day to read words that I hope can inspire you and heal you.

I have no doubt that we have the ability to grow more love and a little less hate.

Let us be the change that we want for our world. Let's smile and laugh a little more.

Let's change our vocabulary to speak more gentle words such as, "I can," instead of

"I should" and "I dislike that," instead of "I hate that." Let's stand up for what we know

is right and be accepting of people even if they are different than us.

Let's make sure that love grows love. Be you... Always!

With love and gratitude,

Lauren Grabois Fischer

Whiskers to Tails! All about Lions (Big Cats Wildlife)

Children's Biological Science of Cats, Lions & Tigers Books

PRODIGYWIZARD
BOOKS